Waiting Together

Danielle Dufayet

illustrated by
Srimalie Bassani

Albert Whitman & Company
Chicago, Illinois

Life is waiting...enjoy every minute!
—DD

To my best friend, Andrea, companion of a
thousand adventures and hilarious WAITS
—SB

Library of Congress Cataloging-in-Publication data
is on file with the publisher.
Text copyright © 2020 by Danielle Dufayet
Illustrations copyright © 2020 by Albert Whitman & Company
Illustrations by Srimalie Bassani
First published in the United States of America
in 2020 by Albert Whitman & Company

ISBN 978-0-8075-0279-2 (hardcover)
ISBN 978-0-8075-0277-8 (ebook)

Printed in China

10 9 8 7 6 5 4 3 2 1 RRD 24 23 22 21 20

Design by Carla Weise

For more information about Albert Whitman & Company,
visit our website at www.albertwhitman.com.

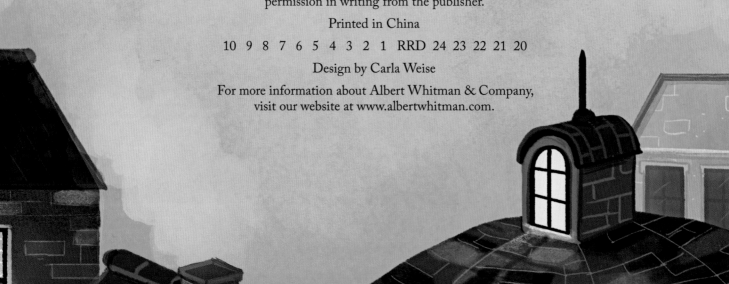

Some waits are still—
like when you wait
for the sunrise,

and it just
magically
appears.

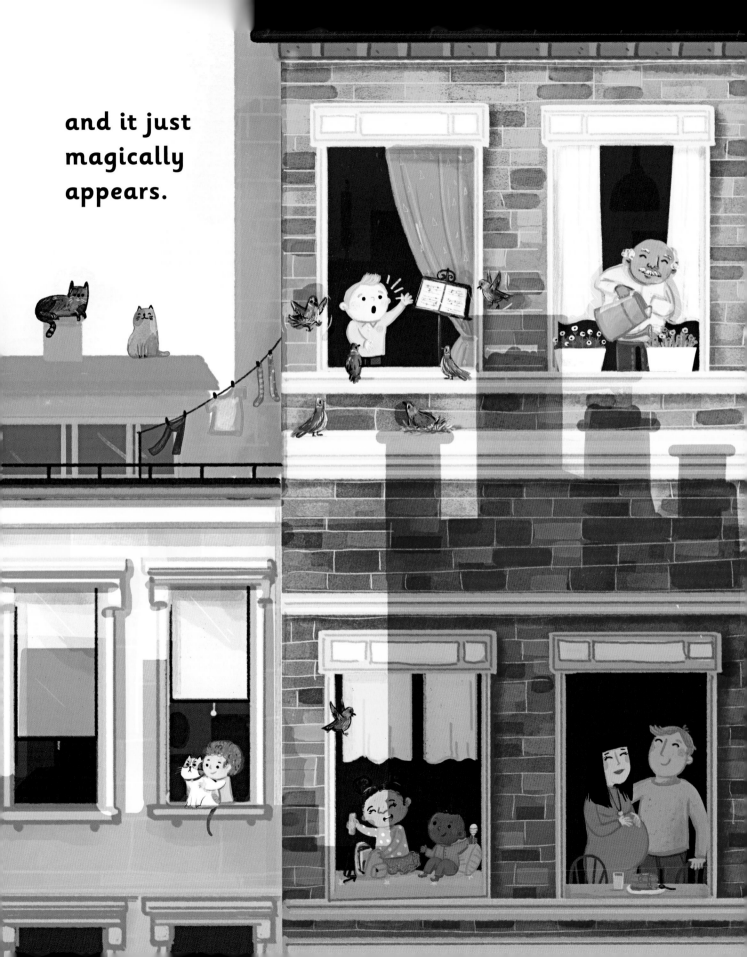

But sometimes waits can
fidget and squirm,

wiggle and jiggle,

or shiver and shake.

Some waits are quick
and pop lickety-split.

Others are slower
and go *clickety-clack*,

drip.

Some waits hide;

others hover;

special ones land right
in your hand!

Sometimes waits go *tick, tick, tick*,

others *ding, ding, ding,*

and once in a while,
waiting can end with a...

KERPLUNK!

**No matter how hard you try...
you can't make waiting go faster;**

if you do, you'll end up with smears, smudges, or breaks.

That's why waiting is always
better with a friend.

Like when you want to fly a kite...
and there's no wind.

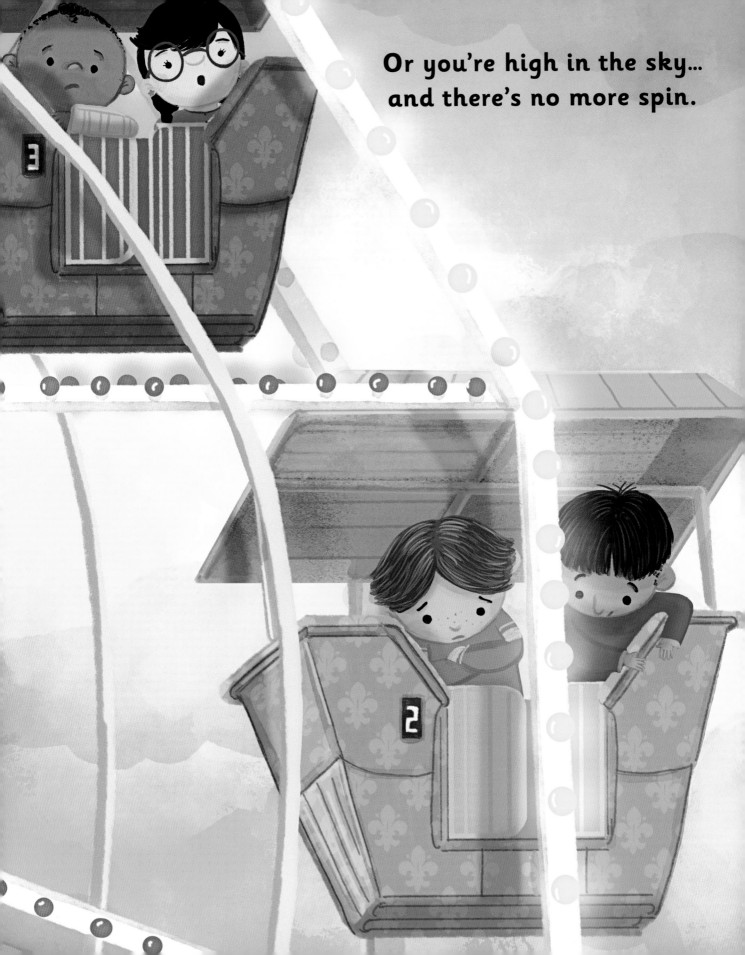

Or you're high in the sky...
and there's no more spin.

At the movies,
waiting can be a long line for popcorn

or teetering on the edge
of your seat.

When it's time
to say goodbye,
you wait as long
as you can...

Some waits are sleepy—
like when you wait for
the very first star,

and it magically
appears...
just in time to
make your wish.

Then, all kinds of waits...

start over again.